D1499265

Tuned Out

written by Mari Kesselring

illustrated by Mariano Epelbaum

12 STORY LIBRARY

www.12StoryLibrary.com

Copyright © 2015 by Peterson Publishing Company, North Mankato, MN 56003. All rights reserved. No part of this book may be reproduced or utilized in any form or by any means without written permission from the publisher.

12-Story Library is an imprint of Peterson Publishing Company and Press Room Editions.

Produced for 12-Story Library by Red Line Editorial

Illustrations by Mariano Epelbaum

ISBN
978-1-63235-039-8 (hardcover)
978-1-63235-099-2 (paperback)
978-1-62143-080-3 (hosted ebook)

Library of Congress Control Number: 2014937411

Printed in the United States of America
Mankato, MN
June, 2014

Table of Contents

Road Trip

Bridget tossed her duffel bag into the back of the minivan. Aunt Katie and Uncle Dan and her cousins Matt and Chloe were already inside, ready to start their trip.

"Do you have your phone?" her dad asked, standing next to the van.

"Yeah, of course," Bridget groaned. She never went anywhere without her smartphone. He knew that. That was one of the reasons her friends called her Bridget Gadget. She always had some sort of tech device with her.

"Okay, be sure to listen to your aunt and uncle," her dad said. "And I know you're really into your new headphones. But please give your ears a break during the drive and talk to your cousins."

Bridget had her high-tech, digital-sound headphones resting around her neck. Her dad understood how much she loved them. In fact, he had helped create them at his tech company, Lingo. The headphones had blue and green LED lights that lit up and pulsed to the beat of whatever song Bridget was listening to. They were also wireless, so no cords got in the way when she was grooving to music being played from her smartphone.

"Yeah, okay. I'll try." Then she scowled and added, "I still can't believe you're making me go."

Bridget and her best friend, Emma, shared the same musical taste. Lately, they were into one band in particular: Crush. Crush was a popular all-girl rock band. They wore colorful outfits and played upbeat music. Both Bridget and Emma knew all the words to every single song. Bridget had even made some mash-ups of their songs on her computer.

Tonight, Crush was finally playing a concert in Cyber Hills. But Bridget would miss it. She'd be on a weeklong road trip to South Dakota with her aunt, uncle, and cousins.

Bridget's dad had told her the trip would be a good chance for her to bond with her cousins. She only got to see them once or twice a year. But Bridget wasn't happy about going on the trip. She felt it was unfair that she had to miss the concert for a stupid road trip. The Crush concert was a once-in-a-lifetime opportunity. Those big stone faces on Mount Rushmore would be there forever.

At least Emma had promised to take a lot of video at the concert with her smartphone so she could show Bridget later. It wouldn't be the same as actually being at the show, but it was better than nothing.

"I know you're upset about missing the concert," Bridget's dad said. "But this trip was planned months ago. Canceling it isn't an option."

Bridget rolled her eyes. "Yeah, I guess."

Knowing that her aunt and uncle had specially planned this trip for her and her cousins didn't make things any better. At least hanging out with Matt was possibly the one thing that almost made Bridget okay with missing the Crush concert. She and Matt had always hung out at family gatherings. He had just finished his freshman year in high school, and Bridget hadn't seen him since the previous summer. He loved music and technology—just like Bridget. He was the only family member who called her by her nickname, Gadget. Matt was always introducing Bridget to cool new music. Now, Bridget was excited to tell him all about Crush.

"Hug?" Bridget's dad put out his arms, and she gave him a quick, stiff hug.

"Just give this trip a chance," he whispered, so no one else could hear. "Who knows? You might have fun."

"Sure," Bridget grumbled. But she doubted it.

"Text me if you need anything."

With that, Bridget clambered into the backseat of the minivan.

"Climb aboard!" Uncle Dan yelled from the driver's seat.

Aunt Katie had taken out the middle seats to fit in a cooler and the family dog, Lola, a springer spaniel with brown spots, who was resting on a big pillow.

The dog is going to be more comfortable than the people, Bridget thought as she took the middle seat in the back. She was sandwiched between Matt and his seven-year-old sister, Chloe.

"Hey," she said to Matt, but he was so busy playing a game on his smartphone that he didn't even look up.

Bridget frowned. Usually, Matt was nonstop talk once they saw each other. But it was a long drive. He was probably as annoyed about going as she was, and they had plenty of time to chat about music.

Chloe acted shy, just as she always did at first. But Bridget knew that in an hour, Chloe would be bugging her to play a game or something.

"Ready to roll?" Uncle Dan called out, turning to look at the three in the back. He smiled broadly and adjusted his sunglasses on his nose.

"Next stop, Mount Rushmore!" Aunt Katie announced from the front passenger's seat in a cheery, light voice.

She was gathering her dark hair into a ponytail. Bridget always thought that her own dark hair was just like Aunt Katie's. They also had the same wide, inquisitive eyes. But even Aunt Katie's upbeat attitude couldn't rescue Bridget from the gloom she felt.

Chloe cheered, and Lola barked in excitement. Bridget shifted uncomfortably, feeling squished between her cousins. Matt didn't even look up.

Battle of the Band

Bridget had covered all the usual topics with her Aunt Katie and Uncle Dan as they shouted from the front seats—"How's summer break going?" "Are you excited for school to start again?" "What's your favorite subject in school?"—within the first half hour of the trip. After that, there wasn't much to say. Chloe kept moving around in her seat and leaning against Bridget, annoying her. Matt kept playing his game.

Bridget had promised her dad that she wouldn't listen to her headphones the whole drive. But she was hopeful that everyone else in the car would want to listen to Crush too. That way, she could do as her dad had asked while still listening to her favorite band.

After a fidgety hour had gone by, Bridget thought she'd give it a try.

"Hey, Matt." Bridget poked her cousin in the ribs. He looked up, seeming annoyed.

"Yeah?" He paused the game he had been playing.

"Have you heard of Crush? The band?" Bridget asked hopefully.

"Crush? Nah, I don't think so."

Bridget smiled widely. She was excited to be introducing her cousin to a new band for a change.

"You're gonna love them." Bridget held out her smartphone toward the front seats. "Aunt Katie? Would it be okay to play some songs off my phone? I really want everyone to hear this band I'm into."

"Sure!" Aunt Katie said. She reached back and grabbed the smartphone from Bridget. Lola raised her head, sniffing curiously.

Unlike her dad's car, the minivan didn't have wireless technology. Aunt Katie had to plug Bridget's smartphone into the car's audio jack so the music could be played through the speakers.

"Play 'The Artifact,'" Bridget told her aunt. "It's the first song."

Bridget smiled at the familiar beat. Then she began to sing along as the lead singer's voice spilled out of the speakers.

Don't tell me about the past.

That's not what I wanna hear.

Let's talk about our future.

Whisper it in my ear.

As the song filled the van, Bridget watched Matt's face to see his reaction. His look of interest quickly turned into a grimace. Bridget worried that he didn't like it.

"This?" Matt finally said. "Really? You like this kind of music now?"

"Well, yeah," Bridget said, feeling embarrassed suddenly.

"Oh my gosh." Matt laughed to himself a little. "I'm sorry, but it's just awful."

Bridget felt her face get hot. Awful? He couldn't really think that. Crush was amazing.

"Mom," Matt complained as "The Artifact" played on, "Can we please listen to something else?"

Aunt Katie gave Matt a stern look over her shoulder. "This is your cousin's favorite band. We can listen to a few songs."

"It's okay," Bridget said quickly. "You can turn it off. I can listen to it on my headphones." She held up her headphones to make a point. Matt was still grimacing, and Bridget suddenly wanted Aunt Katie to turn off Crush as soon as possible. "It doesn't sound right through the car speakers anyway. My headphones have a better sound."

Aunt Katie turned off the music and passed Bridget's phone back to her. As quickly as she could, Bridget put her headphones on and synced them up to her phone so she could drown out everything with Crush's music.

Matt said something to her. She saw his lips moving, but Bridget couldn't hear him.

She was mad at Matt for not realizing how amazing Crush was, and it frustrated her to find that Matt's opinion meant so much to her. Why did it matter what Matt thought? Clearly, his taste had changed since he had started high school—and not for the better.

As she listened to the music, Bridget texted Emma, *Get me outta here. My cousin HATES Crush!*

Oh no! Emma texted back. *Is he human? EVERY1 ♥ Crush!*

What do u think of this outfit? Emma texted. She'd texted a picture of herself in blue jeans with brown boots and a sparkly V-neck tee. *4 the concert.*

Looking at the picture of Emma, Bridget frowned. She couldn't believe she was missing tonight's concert. She wished she were with Emma, picking out her own outfit. But instead, she was trapped in this car with Matt, who had the worst taste in music; Chloe, who was the most irritating seven-year-old on the planet; and her aunt and uncle who were now listening to some boring talk radio station.

There was no way Mount Rushmore would be even half as exciting as the Crush concert. A bunch of old presidents craved into a giant rock? Just boring, Bridget thought.

Bridget felt her eyes water as she looked at the picture of Emma again. She felt so left out.

Looks perfect, she texted Emma. *Wish I could go with.*

Emma texted back, *Wish u could 2! Won't b as fun without u!* Emma sent a picture of herself making a sad face along with the text message.

Bridget replied with a picture of herself looking miserable. At least Emma understood how she felt.

3

Cranking It Up

"Bridget!" Chloe squealed, loud enough that Bridget could hear her even with headphones on. Bridget jumped in her seat, startled, and looked down at Chloe. Chloe held out a blond doll in a pink outfit. Another doll, dressed in purple, lay across Chloe's lap.

Bridget pulled her headphones off and let them rest around her neck.

"Do you want to play?" Chloe asked hopefully.

Bridget suppressed a groan. They'd only been driving for a couple hours. The last thing she wanted to do was become the babysitter on this trip.

"Pleeease?" Chloe whined, poking Bridget in the arm with the hard plastic doll.

Bridget pressed her lips together. If she started playing now, Chloe would be bugging her to play for the whole rest of the trip. She'd better take a firm stand now.

"Sorry, Chloe," Bridget said. "But I really need to listen to my music right now." She pulled her headphones onto her ears again.

Chloe reached over and touched the LED lights on Bridget's headphones as they pulsed to the music.

"Pretty," Chloe said.

"Yeah," Bridget said. "They light up to the music."

"Wow," Chloe breathed. "Can I try? Can you play one of my favorite songs?"

Bridget felt her stomach twist into a knot. She knew she wasn't being a very good older cousin, but she didn't want Chloe using her

headphones. She might break them. So she said, "Yeah, maybe later," but really didn't mean it.

Bridget leaned back in her seat and cranked up the volume on her headphones. Chloe's mouth continued to move, but she finally stopped after she realized Bridget couldn't hear her. Bridget let Crush's "Iced Over" take her away from the cramped car and Chloe's look of disappointment.

After another hour of driving, Bridget felt someone poke her in the ribs. She jumped in surprise. Matt held out his smartphone in his hand. His lips were moving, but all Bridget could hear was Crush singing "Mermaid."

"Wanna play Rocket Blaster?" Matt asked when she'd taken her headphones off. Rocket Blaster was a gaming app that could be played by two people using two separate smartphones. Bridget had played it thousands of times with Emma. She used to enjoy the game, but they'd played it so often that Bridget was kind of bored of it.

"Ah, no thanks," Bridget said. "I've played it too much. I'm sick of that game."

Matt looked puzzled. "How can you be sick of Rocket Blaster? It's the best gaming app there is. Plus they just did an upgraded version. There's more levels."

"I don't know," Bridget said. "The upgrade isn't that much different."

Matt shook his head. "There's no such thing as 'too much' Rocket Blaster. I bet you like Ragin' Rhinos. You do, right?"

Bridget *did* like Ragin' Rhinos, but she wasn't sure how to respond. What if Matt didn't like it and thought she was a loser for liking it? He already thought she was weird for liking Crush and for being sick of Rocket Blaster.

"Um, sure, it's okay," Bridget said finally.

"I know. I love that game," Matt said.

"Me too actually," Bridget said. She was annoyed with herself for not being honest about her opinions in the first place. Who cared if Matt agreed with her or not? Just because he was in high school didn't mean he knew everything.

"Too bad it's not a two-player game," Matt said, looking back to his phone.

"Yeah," Bridget said as she put her headphones back on.

Always Jammin'

With her headphones on and eyes closed, Bridget didn't know they'd gotten off the freeway until she felt the car slow to a stop.

She pulled off her headphones.

"Where are we?" she asked.

"Bathroom break," Uncle Dan explained from the driver's seat.

"Oh, okay." Bridget set her headphones around her neck.

The rest stop was certainly nothing to write home about, Bridget thought. It was a squat brick building in the middle of nowhere, surrounded by open prairie. Inside were bathrooms, maps, and a few vending machines.

Bridget took a picture with her phone and sent it to Emma.

Hello from the middle of nowhere, she texted. Emma didn't text back right away. Probably too busy getting ready for the concert, Bridget thought.

Bridget bought a bag of candy from a vending machine. Maybe sugar would help this drive go faster.

"Oh, Bridget," Aunt Katie said as she spotted Bridget pulling the candy out of the vending machine. "I told you that we have snacks in the car, remember? There's no reason to pay for something here."

"Oh," Bridget said, suddenly feeling guilty about the candy in her hand. "Sorry, I guess I didn't hear you." Bridget had no memory of Aunt Katie talking about snacks or anything else. She must've been listening to Crush.

"That's okay," Aunt Katie said. "But just let me know the next time you get hungry, okay?" She gave Bridget an encouraging smile.

"Yeah, sure," Bridget said.

"We're gonna hang out here for a bit before hitting the road again. Chloe needs to run off some energy before we get back in the car," Aunt Katie explained. "It's hard for little kids to sit still for such a long drive."

Bridget followed Aunt Katie outside. Chloe was running back and forth through the long prairie grasses in front of the rest stop building. She laughed as she ran, her short brown hair bouncing as she bounded through

the prairie. Her bright pink coat flapped behind her as she picked up speed. Matt ran along with her, playing a game or something. Nearby, Uncle Dan walked Lola, her stub of a tail wagging furiously.

Bridget popped on her headphones and sat on a nearby bench. She closed her eyes and just listened to the music.

When they got back in the car, Chloe tugged on Bridget's sleeve.

Bridget removed her headphones.

"Yes?"

"Bridget! Bridget!" Chloe's face was still flushed from her run. Her large, brown eyes glimmered with excitement. "Did you see all those prairie dogs?"

"What?" Bridget asked, puzzled. She hadn't seen any prairie dogs at the rest stop. Of course, she hadn't really been looking either.

"They were hiding in the prairie grass! Didn't you see Matt and me chasing 'em? They were popping out of holes in the ground!"

Bridget had never seen prairie dogs in her life. She wondered what they looked like. Were they cute? Did they really pop out of the ground?

"No," Bridget said. "I guess I missed them."

Forging a Path

"Are we here? Is this it?" Chloe hollered. Bridget could hear her over the music. Even Matt put his hands over his ears.

Bridget looked out the window and saw a sign that read, "Mount Rushmore National Memorial." They had indeed arrived. They were following a line of cars up to the memorial's parking lot.

Everyone in the car was talking excitedly, but Bridget didn't feel like participating. It was almost six o'clock. Crush would be taking the stage back in Cyber Hills in just an hour. Emma was probably standing in line outside the concert hall.

To make matters worse, the battery on Bridget's smartphone was running low. She hoped her uncle and aunt would let her plug it into the car to charge it after they got done at Mount Rushmore. Otherwise, she wouldn't get to see what the concert was like.

Bridget took off her headphones as her uncle parked the van on the top level of the parking ramp. But she kept them around her neck just in case. Chloe would probably find plenty to scream about at Mount Rushmore. From the parking lot, they could get a glimpse of Mount Rushmore off in the distance. Bridget had to admit, it was pretty impressive that people had managed to carve those faces on the side of a mountain.

Bridget was relieved to be out of the car and breathe the fresh air. After sitting for so long, she felt like her legs were made of spaghetti.

"I wanna see Mount Rushmore!" Chloe yelled as she jumped out of the car.

"It's right there!" Aunt Katie said. She pointed out the mountain to Chloe. "We just have to take a little walk to get a better look."

Uncle Dan said he was going to take Lola to the pet exercise area near the end of the parking lot while everyone else took a closer look at Mount Rushmore.

After they passed through the ticket counter and entered into the park, they climbed up to a viewing deck to get a good look at the mountain. Bridget was amazed by the presidents' faces on Mount Rushmore looming above her. They looked like giants peeking out of the rock.

Aunt Karen gathered the group around.

"Okay, Chloe's gonna stick with me, but if you two want to head off on your own to explore, that's okay. Just meet back at the meeting place like we planned."

"Sounds good," said Matt. Bridget nodded. She wasn't sure how she felt about hanging out with Matt. They didn't seem to have much in common anymore. But it was probably better than being stuck with her aunt and shrieking Chloe.

"Come on, Gadget," Matt said as he headed off to the paved path near the mountain. "Let's explore."

"Uh, okay." Bridget followed him, even though she really wanted to check out the gift shop they'd passed on their way in.

"Bye, Bridget!" Chloe called after them from across the park.

As Bridget and Matt trekked along the path around the mountain, Bridget started to regret her decision to follow her cousin. Matt was taller, and he took big strides with his long legs. Bridget could hardly keep up. There were so many people on the path that she kept bumping into other tourists as she struggled to match Matt's pace.

"It's a little crowded," Bridget muttered to Matt.

"Yeah, I know. So many tourists," he remarked. "Here, I've got an idea."

Bridget followed Matt as he stepped off the paved path into the forest alongside it. There was just the hint of trail, probably made by other visitors who had decided to explore off the path.

"Uh, Matt?" Bridget asked, hesitating. "Are you sure we're supposed to leave the trail?"

"Does it matter?" Matt asked. "This will be so much more fun."

"I don't know." Bridget peered into the woods. It seemed like a dangerous idea.

They could get lost pretty easily. "What if we can't find our way back?" she asked.

Matt pulled a bag of cereal, one of the snacks Aunt Katie had brought, out of his pocket. "I'll make a trail with these?" he offered.

"Seriously?" Bridget looked at him skeptically. She pulled out her smartphone and waved it at him. "Remember what happened to Hansel and Gretel? I'm gonna use my Hiker app to track our trail."

When activated, the Hiker app created a map of where you'd traveled on a hike. Then, to go back the way you came, you just consulted the app for directions. Bridget had even used it in big shopping malls to find her favorite stores.

"You really don't need to," Matt said, holding up the bag of cereal again. "I've got this."

Bridget activated the app anyway and followed Matt into the forest.

Drained

They'd been walking through the forest for awhile before Bridget started to get sick of the whole thing. Matt still moved too fast, and now she was bumping into branches instead of people. Mosquitoes were swarming and biting. Plus, they weren't getting a very good view of Mount Rushmore.

Bridget pulled her smartphone from her back pocket and looked at the wavy line it tracked as they walked.

"What are you doing?" Matt whined when he saw her looking at her phone. "I told you we really don't need that."

Bridget looked back at the trail of cereal Matt had left.

"Well," she said. "Even if we don't *need* it, it's fun to use."

"Gadget," Matt said in a lecturing tone. "I know you love your technology. I do, too. But, come on. We're in the forest . . . it's nature. There's no need for your techie stuff here. It's just a distraction. In fact, I left my phone in the car. You really need to unplug sometimes."

Bridget felt she'd put up with a lot from Matt on this trip. He dissed her music and she'd let that go, but now that he was dismissing her tech gadgets, he'd taken one step too far.

"You know what?" Bridget said harshly, wiping sweat from her face. "I've had enough of this. Just because you're older than me doesn't mean you know everything. Stop telling me what to do."

"I never said I knew everything," Matt pointed out.

"But all you do is put down the things I like!" Bridget protested.

"I said I was sorry about the Crush thing," Matt argued. "You just didn't hear me because you've been too busy listening to your dumb headphones the whole trip!"

"Well," Bridget huffed. "Maybe if you were nicer to me I'd actually want to talk to you!"

Matt opened his mouth, but nothing came out. They both stood there staring at each other for a moment. Bridget felt sweat trickle down her back.

Finally Bridget said, "I'm heading back." She whirled around and started back the way they'd come.

As Bridget walked back down the path, she realized she didn't know where or when she was supposed to meet the rest of the family. They must have talked about it in the van, but Bridget, with her headphones on, hadn't heard.

Bridget figured she'd just head back to the visitor center and gift shop area they'd come through to enter the park. The family wouldn't leave without her, so they'd probably wait there. In any case, they'd have to pass through that area to leave the park, so Bridget would see them for sure. If not, she could always call them on her phone.

Bridget followed the directions on her Hiker app until she got to the place where she and Matt had entered the forest. But then, Bridget paused. She couldn't remember which way to go to get back to the visitor center. She'd been letting Matt lead, and he had the map of the park with him. Her Hiker app wasn't any help since she hadn't started tracking their path until after they'd entered the woods. The tourists that had been crowding the path earlier were eerily absent. It was starting to get dark.

But it wasn't a big deal—Bridget still had her smartphone. It couldn't be that difficult to find some helpful directions online.

Bridget sat down on a bench to rest and pulled her smartphone out of her back pocket. The time read 7:30. She imagined Crush on stage back at home in a flurry of colored lights and fog while she sat on a bench in the middle of nowhere. This was *so* wrong.

Bridget used Ami, the voice-command service built into her phone, to figure out where she was. All Bridget had to do was ask something, and Ami would try to find the answer.

"Find map of Mount Rushmore National Memorial," Bridget said into her phone.

"Sorry," said Ami. "I can't complete your request. Try again later."

Bridget frowned. It was such a pain when this happened. Bridget figured the connection was probably weak or overloaded by the other tourists in the area. She tried an online search instead. But she couldn't find any maps that showed all the paths around the park. She also tried her map app, but it couldn't pinpoint her location.

Bridget looked around. She and Matt had traveled pretty far up the trail. Bridget shivered. The temperature was dropping. She didn't have time to keep searching the web.

Bridget sighed. She'd have to call someone for directions. She couldn't call Matt. He had left his phone in the van. Plus, she didn't want to talk to him anyway. She was still mad at him, and it'd be way too embarrassing to admit she'd gotten lost on the tourist path. She searched through the contacts on her phone and found Uncle Dan's number, hoping he'd be cool enough not to tease her for being lost. But just as Bridget hit the green button to make the call, the screen went black.

The phone's battery was dead.

Lost

Bridget stared at her phone's blank screen. She pressed the power button several times, hoping to zap some life back into the device.

"No, no, no, no," Bridget whispered to the phone. "Please . . ."

But there was no denying it. Her battery had just died, and she was lost with no way to contact anyone.

Okay, Bridget thought to herself. Stay calm. It's not like you're in the middle of the Sahara Desert. You're in a national park.

But her heart pounded like a drum inside her chest. She felt lost without her phone. Bridget shivered. It was definitely getting colder. Bridget looked up and down the path again, trying desperately to remember which way she'd taken with Matt when they came up here.

Then Bridget had a thought: as long as she headed down, at least she'd be heading in the right general direction. So, she'd just pick a direction and if the path didn't go downhill, it was the wrong one. Bridget stood up and started along the path.

"Hope this is the right way," Bridget said to herself.

After walking for about 15 minutes, Bridget came across the first sign that she was headed in the right direction. A broken tree branch stretched across part of the path. Bridget remembered stepping over the branch on her way up with Matt.

"Yes!" Bridget cheered to herself. "I'm going the right way!" she yelled into the forest around her. "No thanks to you, Ami," Bridget told the darkened phone in her hand.

As Bridget got farther down the path, she began to see tourists again. And, within the next twenty minutes, Bridget arrived back where she and Matt had started—the main plaza in front of the mountain. She started looking around for Aunt Katie. She scanned the crowds for Chloe's bright pink jacket. Nothing.

Bridget felt a sinking feeling in her stomach. She thought it'd be no problem finding them once she made it to the bottom of the hill, but now she felt nervous. She wished she'd been paying attention when they'd explained what the plan was. What if they planned to meet somewhere *outside* the park?

She reached for her phone to text Emma about what was going on, only to realize all over again the reason she was in this situation.

Bridget wandered into the gift shop, peeking around displays of postcards, guidebooks, and stuffed animals, looking for her family.

"Hey," someone said from behind Bridget. She turned around quickly, hoping for a familiar face. But instead it was a teenage girl employee with blond hair up in a ponytail. "Can I help you find something?"

Yeah, Bridget thought. *My family!*

"Um . . . actually, do you have a phone charger I could use? I sort of got separated from someone and my phone battery died," Bridget said, trying to act as casual as possible. She felt embarrassed to admit she was lost. Little kids like Chloe got lost, not 12-year-olds.

"Sorry, we don't have a charger," the girl said, frowning. "We do have a phone you can use, though."

"That would be great," Bridget said.

"Sure, no problem," the girl said. "There's one behind the counter. Come on."

Bridget followed the teen to a phone hanging on the wall. Bridget tried to remember the last time she'd used a landline. She couldn't.

"Thanks," Bridget said as the employee walked away. Bridget cradled the bulky receiver between her shoulder and cheek. Her fingers hovered over the keypad.

Bridget stared at the numbers. What was she thinking? She didn't know Uncle Dan's number by heart. It was in her contacts list on her now-worthless phone. She didn't know Aunt Katie's or even Matt's number.

In fact, she didn't know Emma's number by heart, and Emma was Bridget's best friend. Bridget started to feel sick to her stomach as she realized that didn't know her dad's number, either.

Tech to the Rescue

Bridget slammed the phone back down on the receiver. She couldn't believe she'd never taken the time to memorize even her own father's phone number. Or her best friend's.

Bridget wandered around the plaza outside the gift shop. She didn't know what to do. She hoped Aunt Katie and Uncle Dan weren't waiting for her somewhere, worrying about her.

Maybe Matt had been right about her listening to Crush on her headphones so much. If she hadn't, she wouldn't be in this mess now. Plus, if she spent more time talking to Matt, maybe she could find some things they had in common instead of only focusing on their differences. Maybe she could even find some common ground with little Chloe too.

The sky was starting to get dark, and even though the park had lights, the dusk seemed to cast shadows over the faces of everyone she passed by, making it even more difficult to pick out her family in the crowd. If Aunt Katie and Uncle Dan were looking for Bridget, they'd probably have a hard time spotting her too. Bridget sat down on a bench at the edge of the plaza. People were gathering around. She heard someone say there was going to be a fireworks display. Bridget watched a dad pick up his daughter and hoist her onto his shoulders so she could see above the crowd.

Bridget's lower lip trembled. She felt as if she were four years old again and lost in the grocery store.

Don't lose it, Bridget told herself. *You're not a little kid. Just stay here, and they'll find you eventually.*

Bridget felt her headphones around her neck. She wished she could listen to music to help her calm down. But with her smartphone battery dead, there was no way she could even do that.

Then suddenly, Bridget thought of something. Her headphones had LED lights that lit up when a song played. But the lights didn't use power from the smartphone to do so. Bridget remembered her dad pointing out the tiny compartment where there was a small battery to power the lights.

"This is the weak part of our design," he had said regretfully. "For the lights to work you have to have a battery here and you have to press the 'on' button on the headphones. It's really just an extra hassle. We've scrapped this in the next model."

If she turned the headphone lights on, maybe Aunt Katie could spot her in the crowd!

Bridget stood up and jumped up onto the bench. She turned her headphones on and the LED lights blazed. With no music playing, they wouldn't flash, but hopefully this would be enough. Bridget held the headphones over her head, waving them back and forth.

Nothing happened at first, but Bridget kept right on waving the headphones. She didn't even care that people were giving her weird looks. This had to work.

Then, just as Bridget's arm started to ache, a little girl in a pink coat burst through the crowd, being chased by two adults.

"Bridget!" Chloe yelled, smiling broadly.

Aunt Katie had her arms around Bridget the minute she stepped down from the bench.

"I'm okay," Bridget quickly assured her aunt.

Peering over Aunt Katie's shoulder, she saw that her Uncle Dan was there too.

"When I heard you and Matt missed the meeting time," he said. "I put Lola back in the van to come look for you."

"I knew it was you!" Chloe said as she tugged on the tail of Bridget's shirt.

"We got worried about you when you didn't meet us at the meeting spot at 8:00," Aunt Katie explained.

"I knew it was her!" Chloe hollered.

Bridget laughed. "Yes, Chloe, you found me!"

"I told them that you were waving your headphones," Chloe explained with a proud smile on her face. "I remembered the lights!"

"I'm really sorry," Bridget said. "I didn't hear where the meeting place was and then my cell phone battery died so I couldn't call you guys. I should've been listening."

"We're just glad we found you," Uncle Dan said. "But where's Matt?"

"Matt?" Bridget looked around. She'd assumed he had already met up with the family. "He isn't with you?"

9

Connecting Again

"No, Matt's not with us," Auntie Katie said as a crease formed in her forehead. "We thought you two were together."

Bridget started to feel sick to her stomach all over again. Was Matt lost too?

Bridget explained to Aunt Katie and Uncle Dan how they'd gotten off the path and went into the forest and then separated almost an hour ago.

"And he doesn't have his cell phone. He left it in the car." Bridget added.

"Let's go back to the meeting spot," Aunt Katie suggested. "Maybe he's waiting for us there."

"Yeah, okay," Uncle Dan said. But they both looked worried.

When they arrived at the meeting spot, a hot dog kiosk just off the main plaza, Bridget was relieved to see Matt waiting there.

"What happened?" she asked.

Matt looked embarrassed. "Uh, I just lost track of time."

"Hmm . . . you would've known the time if you'd had your phone," Bridget pointed out. "Maybe technology does have a place in nature?" she teased.

"Well, I guess," Matt admitted.

"It's okay, Matt!" Chloe interrupted cheerfully. "Bridget got lost!"

Bridget felt her cheeks flush.

"Lost?" Matt raised his eyebrows. "Even with your handy smartphone and magical hiking app?"

"My magical phone . . . magically died," she said, bursting into a giggle. Bridget just had to laugh about it all. She laughed even more when she saw that Matt was laughing too. Maybe they disagreed on some things, and Matt had definitely changed since starting high school, but that didn't mean that they couldn't still be great friends.

Just then, a light came on in the distance. Bridget looked to see that giant spotlights illuminated the famous faces

carved into Mount Rushmore. The white rock itself seemed to glow like the LED lights on Bridget's headphones.

"Wow!" Bridget said.

"That's why we wanted to come here so late," Aunt Katie explained. "It really does look pretty cool."

"Totally," Bridget replied.

"So, what did you think of Mount Rushmore?" Matt asked, when they were back in the car, heading to the hotel.

"Umm . . ." She hesitated. She'd thought the memorial was pretty awesome, but what if Matt didn't feel the same way? But Bridget stopped herself from giving some kind of fake response like "It was okay" or "It was interesting." If Matt liked her at all, he'd at least respect her opinion, even if he didn't agree.

"I thought it was great," Bridget said finally. "What did you think?"

"Yeah," Matt said. "Much cooler than I thought it was gonna be, I have to admit."

Bridget smiled. She felt proud of herself for being honest about her opinions.

"I'm sorry I teased you about the tech stuff," Matt said. "I was just bummed we weren't hanging out more during the drive."

"I'm putting my headphones away now," Bridget said. "At least for most of the ride. Because I really want to hang with you too. I'll even play dolls with Chloe!"

"You will?" Chloe squealed.

Bridget smiled. The next stop on the trip was the Badlands. Maybe she'd have another chance to chase some prairie dogs with Chloe and Matt.

The first thing Bridget did when they got to the hotel that night was to plug in her smartphone. Then she went to her contacts list. She looked up the phone numbers for all the important people in her life—her dad, Emma, Aunt Katie, Uncle Dan, and even Matt. She wrote them all out on a piece of paper and put the paper in her wallet. Now, she'd always have a backup if her phone died. She also thought about asking her dad for a portable charger that she could use in emergencies.

Then Bridget looked through all the text messages she'd missed while her phone was dead. There were a few from Aunt Katie, wondering where she was earlier, and a bunch from Emma.

Emma had sent pictures and video from the Crush concert. Bridget watched the video and looked at all the images. The pictures were a little blurry, but it was clear that it had been an amazing show. Bridget still felt sad that she'd missed it. But she'd had an adventure of her own today.

Looks awesome! Bridget texted Emma.

Emma texted back, *A-MAZ-ING! Wish u could've been there!*

Me 2! But wait til u hear bout Mt. Rushmore!

The End

Think About It

1. Do you think it was fair that Bridget's dad made her go on the trip with her Aunt Katie and Uncle Dan when she wanted to stay home to go to the Crush concert? Why, or why not? Be sure to explain your answer.

2. During the story, Bridget seems to be missing out on important information as she is so focused on listening to her music. How might this story be different had she set aside her headphones? Use examples from the story to explain your answer.

3. Read another Bridget Gadget story. Compare the technology she uses in the two stories. Which of Bridget's gadgets is your favorite? In her stories, do her gadgets more often help her solve problems or create more problems for her? Use examples from the stories to explain your answer.

Write About It

1. Think of a tourist attraction you would like to visit, such as a national memorial like Mount Rushmore or an amusement park. Research the attraction on the Internet or at your local library. Then, use your imagination to write a story about taking a road trip to this destination with your family. Where might you stop along the way, and what things might happen during the trip?

2. Imagine you are either Chloe or Matt. Write about the road trip from the point of view of one of these characters. What would Chloe or Matt think about Bridget's actions during the trip?

3. In this story, Bridget is crazy about Crush. Write about your own favorite singer or band. Describe the singer or band's music and write down why you like this particular singer or band so much. Do you have a favorite song? Write about what the song means to you and why it's your favorite.

About the Author

Mari Kesselring is a writer and editor of books for young people. She's written on various subjects, including William Shakespeare, Franklin D. Roosevelt, and the attack on Pearl Harbor. She is currently pursuing a Master of Fine Arts in Creative Writing at Hamline University. Like Bridget, Mari enjoys technology and new gadgets. She appreciates how technology provides unlimited access to knowledge and brings people closer together. Mari lives in St. Paul, Minnesota, with her husband and their dog, Lady.

About the Illustrator

Mariano Epelbaum has illustrated books for publishers in the United States, Puerto Rico, Spain, and Argentina. He has also worked as an animator for commercials, television shows, and movies, such as *Pantriste, Micaela,* and *Manuelita.* Mariano was also the art director and character designer for *Underdogs,* an animated movie about foosball. He currently lives in Buenos Aires, Argentina.

More Fun with Bridget Gadget

Cyber Poser
A former classmate, Olivia Bates, reconnects with Bridget on her favorite social networking site. But Bridget's not quite sure she remembers Olivia from way back in first grade. Using some online tricks and a new app that her dad's company designed, Bridget sets out to discover whether Olivia is a real friend or just a cyber poser.

Selfie Sabotage
Between schoolwork and tech club and art club, Bridget has little time for fun. When she does finally decide to relax and go to a movie with a friend, she posts a harmless selfie online. That picture, and the lie it reveals, set the stage for another techie problem for Bridget!

Techie Cheater
For her birthday, Bridget gets a pair of high-tech glasses that can receive texts and take pictures. While wearing them, Bridget feels like a secret agent, and she is tempted to use them to cheat on a test, which opens up a whole new world of possibilities . . . and problems.

READ MORE FROM 12-STORY LIBRARY

EVERY 12-STORY LIBRARY BOOK IS AVAILABLE IN MANY FORMATS, INCLUDING AMAZON KINDLE AND APPLE IBOOKS. FOR MORE INFORMATION, VISIT YOUR DEVICE'S STORE OR 12STORYLIBRARY.COM.